*For those who shine bright in the
darkest of times ~ O.H.*

*For Gideon Algernon Mantell (famous historical
palaeontologist) and also his namesake Gideon Algernon
Mantell (my pet dog Algy — who one day may start
digging up old bones himself) ~ S.J.*

tiger tales
5 River Road, Suite 128, Wilton, CT 06897
Published in the United States 2019
Originally published in Great Britain 2019
by Little Tiger Press Ltd.
Text by Owen Hart
Text copyright © 2019 Little Tiger Press Ltd.
Illustrations copyright © 2019 Sean Julian
ISBN-13: 978-1-68010-151-5
ISBN-10: 1-68010-151-X
Printed in China
LTP/1400/2637/0219

For more insight and activities,
visit us at www.tigertalesbooks.com

I LOVE YOU BRIGHTER THAN THE STARS

by Owen Hart   Illustrated by Sean Julian

tiger tales

When sunlight fades and shadows fall,
come walk awhile with me.
We'll watch the sky as stars appear
and count each one we see.

And as we saunter, side by side,
the gentle moon above,
I'll whisper softly just how much
you fill my heart with love.

Look over there! Tonight's first star!
Its twinkle lights our way.
And I will do the same for you—
I'll be your guide each day.

Will there be more? you ask. Oh, yes.
Why don't we climb this hill?
And as we travel, step by step,
our love grows stronger still.

And there it is: a second star!
It shimmers bright and true—
A light that shines forevermore,
just like my love for you.

The third star, near the mountain's peak,
is brighter than the rest.
No matter where you roam, my dear,
you always will be blessed . . .

. . . For even if we're far apart,
we'll wish upon that star,
And sure enough, my love
will find a path to where you are.

At last, we reach the mountaintop
and gasp with pure delight,
For stretching out before us
is an awe-inspiring sight . . . .

The heavens glow with light
as every star comes out to play.
And all at once, we feel more joy
than words could ever say.

Let's take a dip and chase the stars
reflected in the stream.
We leap and splash and giggle
as the dancing waters gleam.

Too many stars to count, you say,
and give a little yawn.
It's time for bed, so home we go
to rest until the dawn.

Let's snuggle up and listen
to the wind's soft lullaby.
I'll kiss your cheek and say good night
beneath our starry sky.

Remember this, my precious one—
you shine so very bright . . . .

I love you more than all the stars
that sparkle through the night.